To Lynn Miller, mother-in-law extraordinaire
and a strong advocate for my books!
—P. Z. M.

I'd like to dedicate this book to my mom who is my best friend
and always there for me—just like the mama bear in this story.
—J. K.

E
456-7072

Wide-Awake Bear
Text copyright © 2018 by Pat Zietlow Miller
Illustrations copyright © 2018 by Jean Kim
All rights reserved. Manufactured in China.

www.harpercollinschildrens.com

ISBN 978-0-06-235603-1 (trade bdg.)

The artist used graphite pencil which she then colored
digitally in Photoshop to create the illustrations for this book.
Typography by Rachel Zegar
17 18 19 20 21   SCP   10 9 8 7 6 5 4 3 2 1
❖
First Edition

Wide-Awake
BEAR

Written by Pat Zietlow Miller   Illustrated by Jean Kim

HARPER
An Imprint of HarperCollinsPublishers

One cold, gray day, Elliott's mother called him inside.

"Time to nap," she said. "We'll sleep 'til spring."

Elliott took a final bite of berries and hurried into their den.

"I miss spring," he said.

So he snuggled into his mother's side, where he slept
and snored.

And dreamed.

Of golden sunshine, soft grass, and budding flowers.

Leafy trees, shady resting spots, and fish-filled streams.

Buzzing bees, just-ripened berries, and warm, sweet honey.

When something tickled his nose, Elliott woke
with a start.

It must be spring!

But the world was dark and dreary.

And his mother was still snoring.

"Oh no!" Elliott whispered. "I should be sleeping."

He lay on his side.

His belly.

His back.

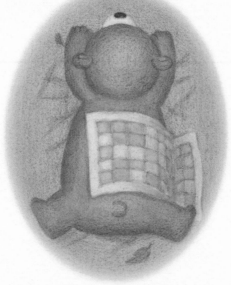

He fluffed the bark strips beneath him
and made a plump pine-needle pillow.

He imagined basking in a sunbeam
and relaxing on a patch of grass.
But nothing worked.
Elliott was . . .

Still.
Wide.
Awake.

He saw things he'd never noticed before.

Strange shadows on the wall.

A dark shape outside.

Elliott rushed to his mother and nudged her with his nose.

She grunted.

He whimpered and whined.

She rolled over and sighed.

Then a gust of wind whirled through the den.

Elliott's teeth chattered. His fur stood on end.

The shadows shifted and seemed to come even closer.

Elliott scampered behind his mother's broad back,
where he shivered and quivered.
And hid.

His mother shook herself awake and scooped
him into a big bear hug.
"What's up, little cub?"

"I didn't sleep 'til spring," Elliott sobbed. "There aren't any blooming flowers, delicious fish, or golden sunbeams. Only shadows and shapes. And I'm . . ."

Still.
Wide.
Awake.

Elliott's mother showed him how the shadows came
from branches.

"We can make shadows too," she said.

So they did. Silly shadows shaped like bees. And trees.
And fish.

Elliott wasn't scared anymore.

So he curled into a ball and shut his eyes. His body
was tired, but his mind was . . .

Still.
Wide.
Awake.

Where were the flowers? And grass? And fish?

Where was spring?

Elliott had to know. So he pretended he was a fish and swam past his mother to the den's entrance.

He saw piles of snow.

Patches of ice.

And thick clouds.

He sighed.

"Spring isn't anywhere."

"There's still time to sleep," his mother agreed.

"But look closer first."

Elliott did. And finally noticed one brave bud.
He remembered his dream.

That bud would become a flower.

Grass waited below the snow.

Fish swam under the ice.

And the sun shone brightly—right behind the clouds.

Spring wasn't gone forever.
It was just asleep.
Like a hibernating bear.

Elliott fluffed his bark-chip bed and plumped his pine-needle pillow.

Then his mother shared one pawful of dried berries and another of cool, sweet honey.

After they'd eaten every bit,
Elliott couldn't help but . . .
YAWN.

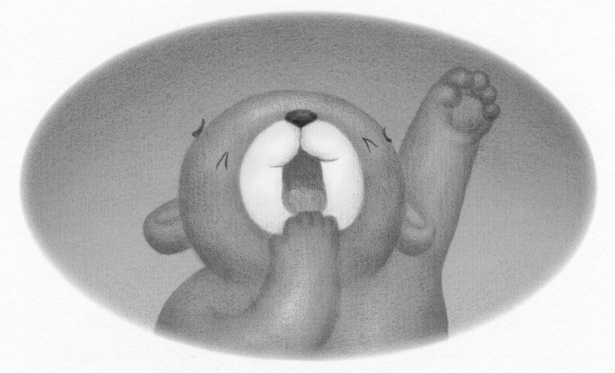

So he snuggled with his mother—who was warmer than the coziest sunbeam.

And, together, they . . .

Slept.
Until.
Spring.